SUPERHERO vs. SCHOOL

WORDS AND PICTURES BY

ETHAN LONG

BLOOMSBURY
CHILDREN'S BOOKS
NEW YORK   LONDON   OXFORD   NEW DELHI   SYDNEY

BLOOMSBURY CHILDREN'S BOOKS
Bloomsbury Publishing Inc., part of Bloomsbury Publishing Plc
1385 Broadway, New York, NY 10018

BLOOMSBURY, BLOOMSBURY CHILDREN'S BOOKS, and the Diana logo are trademarks of Bloomsbury Publishing Plc

First published in the United States of America in July 2020
by Bloomsbury Children's Books

Bloomsbury books may be purchased for business or promotional use. For information on bulk purchases please contact
Macmillan Corporate and Premium Sales Department at specialmarkets@macmillan.com

Library of Congress Cataloging-in-Publication Data
Names: Long, Ethan, author.
Title: Superhero vs. school / by Ethan Long.
Other titles: Superhero versus school
Description: [New York] : Bloomsbury Children's Books, 2020.
Summary: Superhero Scotty is prepared to face any enemy except school, but with true friends by his side,
he can stand up to even this most sinister foe.
Identifiers: LCCN 2019044655 (print) | LCCN 2019044656 (e-book)
ISBN 978-1-68119-828-6 (hardcover) • ISBN 978-1-68119-829-3 (e-book) • ISBN 978-1-68119-830-9 (e-PDF)
Subjects: CYAC: Superheroes—Fiction. | First day of school—Fiction. | Schools—Fiction. | Friendship—Fiction.
Classification: LCC PZ7.L8453 Sw 2020 (print) | LCC PZ7.L8453 (e-book) | DDC [E]—dc23
LC record available at https://lccn.loc.gov/2019044655
LC e-book record available at https://lccn.loc.gov/2019044656

Art created with graphite pencil on Strathmore drawing paper, then scanned and colorized digitally
Typeset in Billy
Book design by Ethan Long and Yelena Safronova • Handlettering by Ethan Long
Printed in China by RR Donnelley, Dongguan City, Guangdong
2 4 6 8 10 9 7 5 3 1

All papers used by Bloomsbury Publishing Plc are natural, recyclable products made from wood grown in well-managed forests.
The manufacturing processes conform to the environmental regulations of the country of origin.

To find out more about our authors and books visit www.bloomsbury.com and sign up for our newsletters.

For Ben Sapp

In brightest day, in darkest night, you'll find our hero racing toward distress . . . and **hurling** himself into **action**!

A morning that began like any other had taken an unexpected turn. For today was not just **any** day— it was the **first day of school**!

But a true hero cannot simply abandon his duties when there are good citizens to protect. School, with its brigade of evil forces, would have to get pushed aside.

To win this nail-biting battle against school, an **ironed shirt** will be useless. Our hero needs a **shirt** made of **iron**!

For at this moment, countless children are about to be swept up in the wrath of the venomous villain!

Our hero has journeyed through **time and space**,
dedicated to **truth and justice for all!**
Minutes mean **nothing** to him!

But time is most certainly running out, as the malevolent villain and her army of minions prepare to **attack**!

. . . our hero takes in the reality of his circumstances.

But just as **our hero** is finally forced to confront his **greatest foe** . . .

And so, in the timeless days that follow, our hero **stands tall**, with his dedication to truth and justice **renewed**!

And as he remembers the villain he once considered to be evil in the most sinister of ways, he feels **empowered**!

For no villain is greater than a team of champions, and heroes are always stronger with true friends by their sides.

And heroes always make the world a safer place!